DESMOND COLE GHOST PATROL

NOW MUSEUM, NOW YOU DON'T

by Andres Miedoso
illustrated by Victor Rivas

LITTLE SIMON

New York   London   Toronto   Sydney   New Delhi

LITTLE SIMON
An imprint of
Simon & Schuster Children's Publishing Division
1230 Avenue of the Americas, New York, New York 10020
First Little Simon paperback edition October 2019
Copyright © 2019 by Simon & Schuster, Inc.
Also available in a Little Simon hardcover edition.
All rights reserved, including the right of reproduction
in whole or in part in any form.
LITTLE SIMON is a registered trademark of Simon & Schuster, Inc.,
and associated colophon is a trademark of Simon & Schuster, Inc.
For information about special discounts for bulk purchases, please contact
Simon & Schuster Special Sales at 1-866-506-1949 or
business@simonandschuster.com.
The Simon & Schuster Speakers Bureau can bring authors to your
live event. For more information or to book an event contact the
Simon & Schuster Speakers Bureau at 1-866-248-3049
or visit our website at www.simonspeakers.com.
Designed by Steve Scott
Manufactured in the United States of America 0819 MTN
2 4 6 8 10 9 7 5 3 1
This book was cataloged by the Library of Congress.
ISBN 978-1-5344-4951-0 (paperback)
ISBN 978-1-5344-4952-7 (hardcover)
ISBN 978-1-5344-4953-4 (eBook)

CONTENTS

CHAPTER ONE

OLD STUFF

Museums are strange. Am I right?

I mean, museums are like big buildings filled with old stuff you're not allowed to touch. They have old paintings and old statues. Old furniture and old jewelry. They even have old pottery.

That's kind of like leaving your icky, dirty dishes lying around for a hundred years! Don't get me wrong. Museums might have new art too. But I never really understand it. Like, which side is up? And is that supposed to be a horse?

Anyway, we didn't come to the Kersville Museum that day to see art. We came to see old people!

No, I'm not talking about your grandparents or great-grandparents. Or even great-*great*-grandparents. I'm talking about *really* old people.

Yeah, I'm talking about *mummies*! You know mummies, right? They are wrapped in cloth, surrounded by gold, and live in pyramids for thousands of years. Yeah, of course you know what a mummy is.

Because mummies are the coolest!
Well, that's what I used to think.
Right now, I'm having some really
serious doubts.

That's me, Andres Miedoso. I'm the one on the back of the yak. Well, a fake yak.

That's my best friend, Desmond Cole. He's in the chariot. The chariot is real, but the horse is fake.

DESMOND COLE

ANDRES MIEDOSO

No, your eyes aren't playing tricks on you. The yak and the chariot *are starting to move*! As a matter of fact, everything in the whole museum is turning real.

My mom likes to say that museums make history come to life. I don't think this is what she meant!

Oh no, my yak is taking off. I better hold on tight!

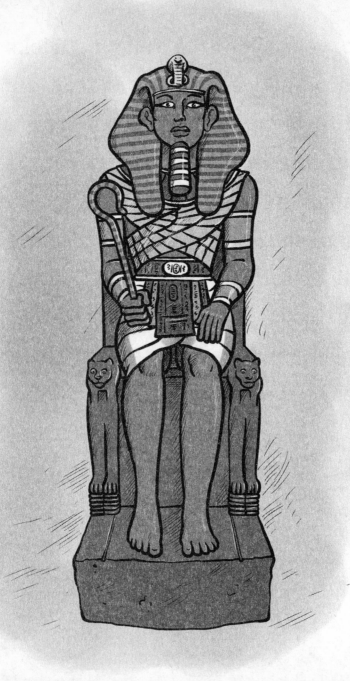

CHAPTER TWO

THE FOREVER AND EVER KING

I guess I should start by telling you a little story. I used to think it wasn't true, but after reading this, you will have to judge for yourself.

More than four thousand years ago, there was a king who called himself the Forever and Ever King.

He wanted to live forever.

Crazy, right?

I don't want to spoil the ending, but let me say this, he definitely didn't live forever and ever. Nope.

But his family went ahead and made him into a mummy, and they put him in a special place where he

could stay for eternity. That's just a fancy way of saying forever and ever.

The family decorated the mummy's chamber with gold statues and pots filled with honey. They even gave him a giant bed shaped like a bigger version of himself to sleep in!

I know what you're thinking. You want to know why I had to tell you a story that was four thousand years old. You're probably wondering what any of that has to do with me and Desmond.

Well, I'll tell you.

A few weeks ago, the Kersville Museum held a contest to celebrate some silly mummy that was going to be at the museum this weekend. To win free passes, kids had to draw and color a very special mummy chamber.

And guess who won?

Desmond Cole, of course!

He drew one with ghosts, sleep-walking snowmen, monsters, and mersurfers. People thought he had a big imagination, but I knew that he had met every creature in his drawing. Still, it was a good drawing.

Desmond also included a lot of food. He had pizzas, cheeseburgers, tacos, candy bars, and even s'mores! I guess if I were a mummy, I'd want to live there for eternity too.

So anyway, Desmond won the free tickets.

And that's why we were at the museum on what was probably the craziest day ever!

TYRANOSAURUS REX

CHAPTER THREE

SCARY BUTTERFLIES

Museums also have scary things. Not ghost scary, but real-life scary.

They have dinosaur bones that are so huge that they reach the roof of the building. And they have all kinds of animals on display—lions and bears and wolves (and yes, yaks).

I know the animals are stuffed and made to look like they were still alive. But that never stopped me from being a little jumpy! Okay, from being *very* jumpy.

I know, I know. I will admit that it doesn't make sense. Until you remember that Kersville is haunted.

You never really know what could happen here.

Desmond's mom and dad were really nice to bring us to the museum that day. When we stepped inside the building, the first thing we saw was a giant grizzly bear with its huge fangs and claws showing. It looked like it was trying to grab us!

GRIZZLY BEAR

"Oh my!" Desmond's dad said, gasping. "That looks so real."

Mrs. Cole took him by the hand. "It's just a display," she explained. "There's nothing to be scared of."

I knew what she was saying was true. That bear couldn't hurt us, but that didn't stop my heart from beating at triple speed. I moved away from it as fast as I could.

That was when Mrs. Cole pointed to a line, the one every parent spots.

No, it wasn't the line for the bathroom!

It was the line for the butterfly exhibit.

"Would you boys like to see the butterflies?" Mrs. Cole asked us.

"I just want to get to the mummy already!" Desmond said excitedly. He was wearing a funky explorer hat for some reason. When Desmond dresses up like that, it means he's really excited. And today he was

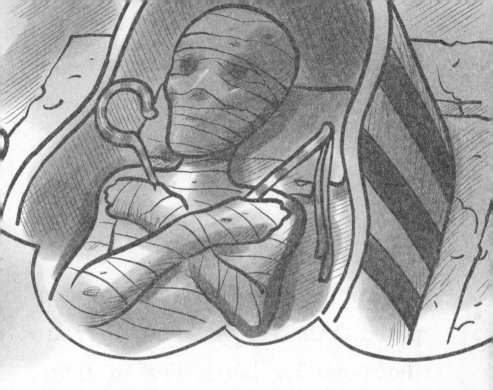

really excited about mummies.

I wasn't as excited. I mean, the butterfly exhibit sounded kind of cool. And totally safe. "Let's go see the butterflies," I told Desmond. "We can see the mummies later."

I don't know why, but now that we were at the museum, I was getting nervous to see the mummies. Reading about them was fun, but being this close to the real ones was a little scary.

Desmond turned to me and whispered, "Andres, you know there are thousands of butterflies in there, right?"

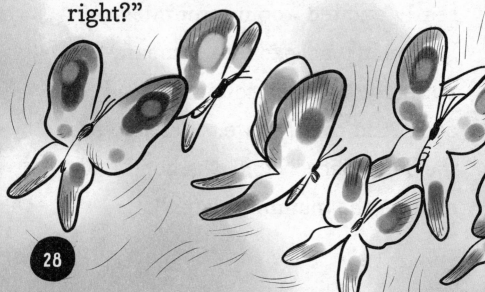

I gulped. *"Thousands?"*

He nodded. "Yep. And all those butterflies will be flying around the room at the same time."

That sounded like . . . *a butterfly tornado*!

Suddenly, the thought of a creepy
mummy sounded less scary than
being stuck in a room with a swarm
of butterflies.

"Um, I'll stay with Desmond," I told Mr. and Mrs. Cole. "We want to see the mummy that is not going to move at all."

"Suit yourself," Mrs. Cole said as she waved to the security guard. "Mr. Roberts, will you keep an eye on Desmond and Andres while we're in the butterfly exhibit?"

Mr. Roberts nodded. He was an older man in a gray uniform. His curly white hair stuck out from under his security hat.

"Oh, of course, Mrs. Cole," the guard said. "Don't worry about the kids. This museum is the safest place in the world."

Boy, oh boy, was he wrong!

CHAPTER FOUR

MUMMIES THE WORD

While most of the parents went to see the butterflies, Desmond and I walked through the museum on our way to the mummies exhibit. We passed through the art room, which seemed to be where all the rest of the grown-ups were.

They were staring at the art as if they were under a spell.

Desmond and I looked at the new art for a little while. And as usual, none of it made sense. There were paintings that looked like something I finger painted when I was in kindergarten, and a squiggly sculpture that seemed more like painted spaghetti. And there was even a painting of a woman who had ten eyes . . . all on one side of her face!

"Why don't artists ever paint pictures of ghosts?" Desmond whispered to me.

"Probably because ghosts are invisible," I whispered back.

Desmond nodded. "Good answer," he said as he grabbed my arm. "Come on. We have to find the mummy king."

He was right. After all, it was why we were there.

So we kept moving through the museum into a room filled with old statues. They were huge and so real-looking.

"This one looks like you," said Desmond with a laugh. The statue did look a little like me . . . if I carried a sword and had a ton of muscles!

"This one looks like you," I said, pointing to a statue of a guy riding a chariot.

"I would never know how to drive one of those things!" Desmond said.

As we left our statues behind, we passed a really creepy mask. Desmond and I had seen that mask before, when we were hunting for monsters. But that was a whole other story!

Desmond leaned closer to me and whispered, "Remember this creepy guy? I still think that mask is haunted."

Before I could respond, the mask actually started talking. In a deep voice, it said, "Desmond Cole, you are right. I *am* haunted."

The tiny hairs on the back of my neck stood up, and I was about to faint when Mr. Roberts popped out from behind the mask.

"Sorry, kids," he said with a laugh. "I couldn't help myself, especially when I heard you talking about this mask."

I let out a whimper. "So it's not haunted?" I asked him.

"Of course not," Mr. Roberts said. "The only thing haunted in this place are the snacks in the vending machine. I wouldn't eat any of those

if I were you. They're so old that I bet they are potato-chip mummies by now."

"Thanks for the tip, Mr. Roberts," Desmond said. "Now, we've got a mummy we need to see!"

On the way to the mummy exhibit, we stopped to check out the vending machine. Mr. Roberts was right. Nobody had gotten a snack from it in a long time. There were cobwebs on the inside. Plus, the snacks were so old that I'd never heard of them before.

"Doodle Birds?" I said, reading the label on one of the bags. "Who would eat something called Doodle Birds?"

But I knew who would: Desmond Cole! That kid would eat anything if it wasn't made by his parents!

I was pretty sure cobwebs, weird names, and stale food wouldn't stop Desmond if he was hungry enough, so I grabbed him.

"Let's go," I said, pulling him away from the vending machine. We were there to see a mummy, not eat Doodle Birds!

CHAPTER FIVE

WAKE UP, SLEEPYHEAD

Stepping into the mummies exhibit was like going back in time. *Way back!* Like more than four thousand years ago. The whole thing was set up to look exactly like the Forever and Ever King's final resting place.

Sounds creepy, right?

I thought so too. But you know what? It was actually supercool.

There were gold statues everywhere, and for some reason, most of them were cats. And there were giant painted pots that surrounded the mummy king.

Along the walls the museum had even displayed the winning drawings from the contest. It was easy to spot Desmond's drawing. It was the one with all the haunted stuff and food on it!

The mummies exhibit was pretty crowded, so it took us a little while to make our way up to the actual mummy king. It was in a long glass case, and it was a lot bigger than I thought it was going to be.

Desmond and I got as close as we could. The mummy king was wrapped from head to toe, and it was lying in an opened box with lots of fancy paintings on it.

"The box is called a sarcophagus," Desmond told me.

"A sar-coff-a-*what*?" I asked.

"Sarcophagus," Desmond repeated. "It's like a coffin for a mummy."

Sometimes Desmond knew the strangest things.

As we stood there, a bad feeling washed over me. Yeah, the mummy king was behind glass, but it was still a mummy.

How did I let Desmond talk me into coming here? Don't mummies have curses? Why did Desmond always have to love the creepiest things in the world?

Suddenly, all I wanted to do was get out of there.

"I—I'm ready to leave," I said.

"Relax," Desmond told me. "It's not like this mummy is cursed or anything."

And that's when I heard it: a low voice that rumbled to life.

"M-m-m-mummy is cursed," the voice growled.

I screamed a high-pitched scream. And I jumped a high jump.

And I fell into one of the huge ancient pots. It teetered. And tottered. And all I could think about was how I was going to break something that had already survived for thousands of years.

Mr. Roberts suddenly popped out from hiding behind the mummy's glass case.

"I got it!" he said as he caught the pot. "Oh, there I go again. I'm sorry

for pranking you a second time. Maybe I shouldn't have made that silly mummy voice. I had no idea your friend was so easily scared, Desmond."

As Mr. Roberts set the pot back in place, something slimy oozed out of it, dripping right onto the floor. It made the whole room smell like the sweetest honey ever.

"Oh no. I better clean up that ancient honey," Mr. Roberts said, looking at the puddle. "Wouldn't want anyone to slip on that. I'll go get a mop."

When he left, Desmond shook his
head. "Don't mind Mr. Roberts," he
said. "He loves trying to scare kids."

But I knew that nothing scared Desmond Cole. Well, at least, nothing that we had found yet.

CHAPTER SIX

HONEY TRAP

As I carefully stepped over the spilled honey, I found myself face-to-face with a different mummy case. It was standing so still that I wanted to be completely quiet.

But the supersweet smell of the honey was filling the air.

It made me want to sneeze. I held it in.

And that was when I saw something strange.

I saw the mummy case move . . . just a little. But that was impossible!

Only thing was that it happened again. The mummy's door slowly creaked as it opened wider. A hand reached out. Then I saw its fingers move too. A little cloud of dust puffed up around them. Finally, the mummy's arm stretched from the sar-coff-a-thingy, and that was it for me. I didn't need to see anything else.

I was out of there!

I grabbed Desmond and said, "We need to leave. *Now!*"

As I pulled him away from there, I probably should have looked where I was going because the next thing I knew, I was slipping and sliding in that spilled honey puddle.

How could something that smelled so sweet be so sticky and gross? Ugh. I wiped as much as I could off my jeans, and when I stood up to grab Desmond again, he wasn't next to me. He had found the mummy king.

And since it was Desmond, he wasn't running away like I was. Oh no way! Desmond rushed right up to that mummy and said, "Hello, King. My name is Desmond Cole."

But the mummy didn't seem like it wanted to make friends. Its jaw moved slowly under all that wrapping, and a sound came out.

"Doo . . . doo."

I whispered to Desmond, "Did that mummy say what I think it said?"

But Desmond wasn't paying any attention to me. He leaned closer to the mummy and said, "No, my name is Desmond."

But the mummy just kept saying "doo . . . doo." It made no sense. But mummies that come alive don't need to make sense, I guess.

The ancient Forever and Ever
King crawled out of its glass case.
Then other mummies crawled out of
their cases too!

And yes, every kid in the room

saw them. I mean, seeing mummies walking around is definitely not normal, even in Kersville.

So the kids did what any normal kid would do.

They screamed. And yes, so did I!

CHAPTER SEVEN

THINGS GET REAL

EEEEEEK!

AAAAGH! EWWW!!

Here is something I've learned about mummies: They do not like screaming children!

That mummy king chased kids right out of the exhibit hall. Well, it *slow* chased us. I learned this too: Mummies do not move fast.

Try wrapping yourself up from head to toe and see how fast you can run!

But it didn't matter how slow it was. We were being chased *by a mummy*, and we needed to get away.

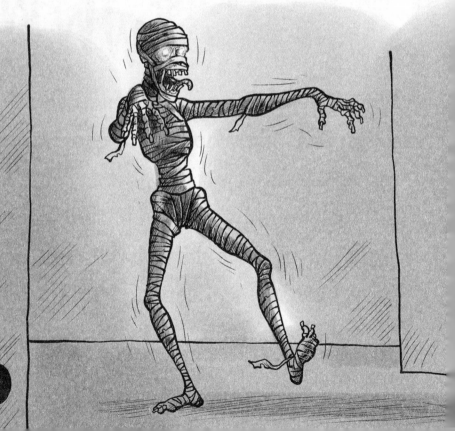

As we ran through the other rooms, Desmond asked, "Do you smell something sweet?"

I sniffed the air. "That's the honey," I said. "Some of it must still be on my jeans."

"Interesting" was all Desmond said back to me.

SNIFF
SNIFF

SNIFF
SNIFF

"Hold up," I said as we turned a corner. "Are we really going to talk about honey when there's a true-life mummy chasing us?"

Sometimes Desmond had a way of forgetting what was really important.

Desmond ignored my question and said, "You know, they say that the Forever and Ever King's honey was cursed."

"Cursed how?" I asked.

"The honey was supposed to give life to a mummy," he told me.

"Looks like the curse worked!" I snapped.

If only Mr. Roberts hadn't scared us like that. If only the museum had put those pots of honey behind a glass wall.

If only the mummies had stayed put in the sar-coff-a-whatever-it's-called!

But of course, things are never that simple in Kersville!

I had been lost in all my thoughts when the sound of a slow-moving mummy was replaced by the sound of more footsteps...*heavy* footsteps!

I didn't want to turn around because I didn't want to know what else was behind us.

"Um, Desmond," I whispered. "Does that cursed honey only give life to mummies?"

"I'm not sure," he said. And we stopped to see what was there.

The statues from earlier were all staring back at us. Only now, they had come to life.

CHAPTER EIGHT

THE GIFT SHOP

THUD·THUD

My feet knew what to do before I did.

They ran!

Now, if you think mummies are slow, you should see how slow stone statues run.

They were so big and heavy, it took them forever to move.

Every step that thick marble rock took, we heard a **THUD**.

My feet and I ran through the old art room where every painting had come to life too. The horses were galloping. The

people were sitting at the kitchen table, eating. The ballet dancer was, well, you get it!

But we didn't stop there. We dashed into the modern art room, and all of a sudden, the red drippy painting started dripping onto the floor. The weird squiggly sculpture thingy straightened itself out. And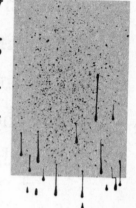

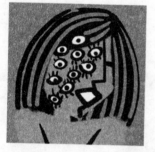 a painting with ten eyes said, "Well, well, well. Look at this piece of art. It's called *Two Boys Running*."

I stopped running. *Is the painting talking about us? It's not like we are a piece of art! Are we?*

I didn't have time to argue with that weird painting. Desmond and I ran to the front part of the museum where the animal and dinosaur bones used to be. But they were gone!

I looked around. "Where are the bones?" I asked Desmond. "They were just here!"

Oh, I wish I had never asked *that* question.

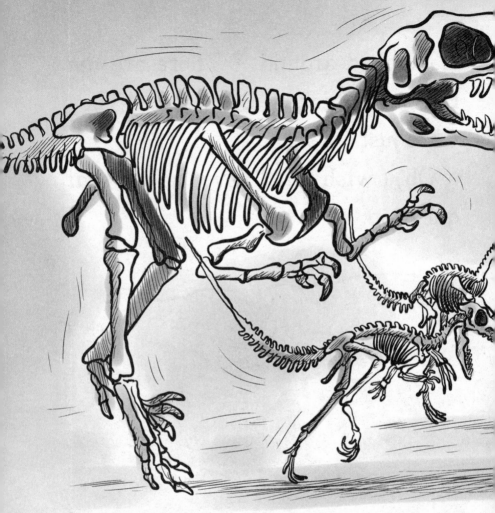

Out of the shadows the animal and dinosaur bones marched into the center of the room. Right toward us!

And the bones were nothing like mummies and statues.

They moved fast!

Desmond and I were surrounded. The front doors were blocked by the bones of the saber-toothed tiger.

The door to the butterfly exhibit was blocked by the bones of the mammoth.

Even the door to the bathroom was blocked by that giant mask. It was like they were trying to trap us!

Then the museum grew quiet, and the only sound we heard was the mummy king walking and saying, "Doo . . . doo."

My heart raced. I was ready to give up when Desmond whispered, "I have a plan."

He grabbed my arm and pulled me into one of the best places at the museum: the gift shop!

CHAPTER NINE

TOILET PAPER PLAN

"Desmond! Now isn't the time to shop," I whisper-screamed.

"Dude, I'm not shopping," he whisper-screamed back. "I told you that I've got a plan!"

Desmond waved me over toward the back of the gift shop.

There was a bathroom. We snuck inside. Of course, I went straight for the window, where I hoped to make a quick escape. But not Desmond. He went into a stall.

Did he forget we are being chased by a mummy? And statues? AND a bunch of bones?

"Desmond," I whisper-screamed again, a little louder. "Now is not the time to go to the bathroom!"

"Dude, I'm just getting this," he said, holding up a roll of toilet paper. "It's part of my plan."

A few minutes later Desmond and I walked back through the gift shop. Except now we were wrapped from head to toe in toilet paper, mummy style.

As we walked past the stuffed animals and toys in the store, they started to come to life. I mean, this was getting out of control!

We left the gift shop and ran smack-dab into you-know-who: the mummy king!

Desmond waved hello again, but this time he said, "Doo . . . doo."

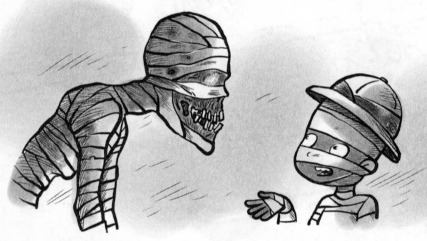

"What are you doing?" I hissed.

"Trying to talk to it," Desmond whispered. He turned back to the mummy and repeated, "Doo . . . doo."

The mummy looked at us hard, like it was trying to figure us out. The next thing we knew, it pulled on our toilet paper, sending us spinning like two giant tops!

Talk about getting dizzy!

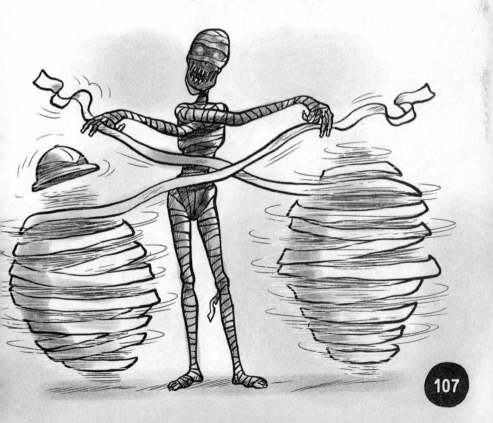

By the time we stopped spinning, the mummy was heading for the front door. "It's trying to escape!" I screamed.

Desmond sprang into action. "We have to stop him!" he said.

And that's when we did the only thing we could think of. I jumped on a yak, and Desmond jumped into a chariot.

Well, it seemed like a good idea at the time.

CHAPTER TEN

SNACKS FOR MUMMY

It didn't take long for me to figure out that it's not easy to ride a yak. Desmond couldn't ride his chariot either. Between the two of us, we had no idea what we were doing!

But I grabbed the mummy's wrapping and held on tight!

That mummy king dragged me
around until it slammed into the old,
dusty vending machine.

Suddenly, all the fake animals in the museum returned to their spots and went right back to being fake again. The dinosaur bones and the statues and everything that had come alive went back to being . . . well, normal.

Everything except the mummy. It stared into the vending machine and a smile spread across its face. The Forever and Ever King said, "Doo . . . doo . . . Doodle Birds!"

Desmond ran over and pointed to the Doodle Bird chips in the vending machine. "You want those?" he asked the mummy.

The mummy nodded slowly. Then Desmond pulled out some change and bought the chips for it.

When he handed over the bag, the mummy said, "Thank you."

I never thought I'd see anything like that! Then the mummy walked back to its exhibit. When it got there, it ripped open the chips, dipped a Doodle Bird into the spilled honey, and chomped them down . . . fast.

"See?" Desmond said. "It was just hungry. I understand. I get like that when I'm hungry too."

I couldn't believe my eyes. That mummy really seemed to like those super-old, stale Doodle Birds!

When it was done, the mummy laid back down in its sarcophagus and that was it. The adventure was over. The other mummies went back to their places too.

All the kids at the museum cheered for me and Desmond, just as parents came out of the butterfly exhibit.

Finally, Mr. Roberts showed up with a mop and a bucket. "Hmm, that's weird," he said. "All the honey has been cleaned up. Did I miss anything while I was gone?"

Desmond and I glanced at each other quickly, but we didn't say anything. No way would he believe us if we told him what really happened!